Louise Pearson was born and raised in Farnborough Hampshire. She has always had a flair for poetry and has written for memorials and friends. She is married and a mum to two beautiful children, who are her greatest accomplishment. She loves spending her spare time taking family days out and trips to the cinema.

THE BUG CIRCUS

BY LOUISE PEARSON

AUSTIN MACAULEY PUBLISHERS™
LONDON • CAMBRIDGE • NEW YORK • SHARJAH

ISBN 9781398406667 (Paperback)
ISBN 9781398406674 (ePub e-book)

www.austinmacauley.com

First Published 2022
Austin Macauley Publishers Ltd®
1 Canada Square
Canary Wharf
London
E14 5AA

For my greatest accomplishments,
Jessica and Benjamin.

Thank you Stuart, for being you.

Thank you to the girls at work for
the encouragement.

Thanks to my mum for making me who I am and
thank you to Austin Macauley for believing in me.

Have you ever wondered...
What life would be like for a bug?
Well, let's go and meet the circus ant,
Who goes by the name of Doug!

He would travel around the country,
In each town, he'd build a ring
Where bugs could come and watch some tricks,
And to even see some sing!

The ringleader, he was a big lad,
A huge stag beetle, went by the name of Bob.
He loved making all the bugs happy
So he took a lot of pride in his job.

He would introduce the singing ladybird,
She would bring in the crowds for miles!
And the earwig clowns would mess around,
To give the crowd great big smiles.

The amazing transforming caterpillar,
Would leave the crowd super dazed
As by end of the show, he completely changed,
Leaving them all amazed!

For he had become a butterfly,
Such a beauty, what a wonderful sight!
He would fly to the roof of the big top,
Showing off his wings in flight.

And then there were the woodlice,
Who happened to be sister and brother.
The pair were great performing acrobats,
And they would never ever drop each other!

They would swing high up on the trapeze
And balance along some wire!
They would somersault through the air
And even jump through hoops of fire!

Now Doug had a brother called Dave
Who happened to be the circus strongman!
He could lift most things over his head
Even Doug's home – his caravan!

And the final part of the show,
Was a dance by a spider called Tina.
She was so beautifully graceful,
And was such a talented ballerina!

She would twist and turn and jump around,
All with such beauty and grace,
She would tie her hair up in a bun,
Whilst wearing a tutu of lace!

The audience of bugs would stand and cheer,
At the end of every show.
Then the ants would pack up the tent again,
And on to the next town they'd go!

So if you see an ant walking by,
Maybe watch to see where he might go.
He might lead you along to the Bug Circus
So you too can watch the show!